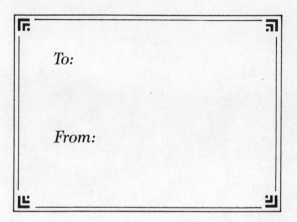

To:

From:

Christmas
T·I·D·I·N·G·S

EDITED BY
Louise Bachelder

WITH ILLUSTRATIONS BY
Wendy Watson

PETER PAUPER PRESS, INC.
WHITE PLAINS • NEW YORK

MAY the blessed light be on you, light without and light within. May the blessed sunlight shine on you and warm your heart until it glows like a great fire, so that a stranger may come and warm himself at it, and also a friend.

May God always bless you, love you, and keep you.

AN ANCIENT BLESSING

Cover Design: J. O'NEILL

Christmas
T·I·D·I·N·G·S

God bless us every one, prayed Tiny Tim,
   Crippled and dwarfed of body, yet so tall
Of soul, we tiptoe earth to look on him,
   High towering over all.

James Whitcomb Riley

I will honor Christmas in my heart, and try
to keep it all the year.

Charles Dickens

He that is of a merry heart hath a continual
feast.

Proverbs 15:15

He that proclaims the kindnesses he has received, shows his disposition to repay them if he could.

MIGUEL DE CERVANTES

Some say, that ever 'gainst that season comes,
Wherein our Saviour's birth is celebrated,
This bird of dawning singeth all night long;
And then, they say, no spirit dare stir abroad,
The nights are wholesome, then no planets
    strike,
No fairy takes, nor witch hath power to
    charm,
So hallow'd and so gracious is the time.

WILLIAM SHAKESPEARE

Kindness in words creates confidence,
Kindness in thinking creates profoundness,
Kindness in giving creates love.

LAO-TSE

I thank God, who has made me poor, that He has made me merry.

SYDNEY SMITH

7

GREAT is the man who does not lose his child's
heart.

MENCIUS

O THE snow, the beautiful snow,
Filling the sky and the earth below.
Over the house-tops, over the street,
Over the heads of the people you meet,
    Dancing,
    Flirting,
    Skimming along,
Beautiful snow, it can do nothing wrong.

JOHN WHITTAKER WATSON

    WHAT in me is dark
Illumine, what is low, raise and support;
That to the height of this great argument
I may assert eternal Providence,
And justify the ways of God to men.

JOHN MILTON

WHEN we climb to Heaven, 'tis on the rounds
of love to men.

JOHN GREENLEAF WHITTIER

GOD's love gives in such a way that it flows from a Father's heart, the well-spring of all good. The heart of the giver makes the gift dear and precious; as among ourselves we say of even a trifling gift, "It comes from a hand we love," and look not so much at the gift as at the giver.

MARTIN LUTHER

LOVE came down at Christmas,
Love all lovely, Love Divine.
Love was born at Christmas;
Star and angels gave the sign.

. . . . . .

Love shall be our token,
Love be yours and love be mine, —
Love to God and all men,
Love the universal sign.

CHRISTINA ROSSETTI

EVERY gift which is given, even though it be small, is in reality great, if it be given with affection.

PINDAR

WE thank Thee for this place in which we dwell; for the love which unites us; for the peace that is accorded us; for the hope with which we expect the morrow; for the wealth, the work, the food and the bright skies that make our lives delightful; for our friends in all parts of the earth, and our earthly helpers in this land. Help us to repay in service one to another the debt of Thine unmerited benefits and mercies.

ROBERT LOUIS STEVENSON

THERE can be prayers without words just as well as songs, I suppose.

GEORGE DU MAURIER

To worship rightly is to love each other, each smile a hymn, each kindly deed a prayer.

JOHN GREENLEAF WHITTIER

WE never know what ripples of healing we set in motion by simply smiling on one another.

HENRY DRUMMOND

Not believe in Santa Claus? You might as well not believe in fairies. . . . No Santa Claus! Thank God, he lives and he lives forever. A thousand years from now, Virginia, nay, ten times ten thousand years from now, he will continue to make glad the heart of childhood.

FRANCIS PHARCELLUS CHURCH

To LIVE is not to live for one's self alone; let us help one another.

MENANDER

It is a comely fashion to be glad;
Joy is the grace we say to God.

JEAN INGELOW

HEAVEN may have happiness as utterly unknown to us as the gift of perfect vision would be to a man born blind. If we consider the inlets of pleasure from five senses only, we may be sure that the same Being who created us could have given us five hundred, if He had pleased.

CHARLES CALEB COLTON

DESIRE joy and thank God for it. Renounce it, if need be, for others' sake. That's joy beyond joy.

ROBERT BROWNING

IT was always said of him, that he knew how to keep Christmas well.

CHARLES DICKENS

AMID my list of blessings infinite,
Stands this the foremost "That my heart has bled."

EDWARD YOUNG

A GOOD conscience is a continual Christmas.

BENJAMIN FRANKLIN

MEAT eaten without either mirth or music is ill of digestion.

SIR WALTER SCOTT

THEY who have steeped their souls in prayer
Can every anguish calmly bear.

RICHARD MONCKTON MILNES

WHO can be insensible to the outpourings of good feeling, and the honest interchange of affectionate attachment, which abound at this season of the year? A Christmas family-party! We know nothing in nature more delightful! There seems a magic in the very name of Christmas. Petty jealousies and discords are forgotten. . . . Kindly hearts that have yearned towards each other, but have been withheld by false notions of pride and self-dignity, are again reunited, and all is kindness and benevolence! Would that Christmas lasted the whole year through (as it ought), and that the prejudices and passions which deform our better nature, were never called into action among those to whom they should ever be strangers!

CHARLES DICKENS

OUR prayers should be for blessings in general, for God knows best what is good for us.

SOCRATES

IN the pursuit of happiness half the world is on the wrong scent. They think it consists in having and getting, and in being served by others. Happiness is really found in giving and in serving others.

HENRY DRUMMOND

CHRISTMAS! 'Tis the season for kindling the fire of hospitality in the hall, the genial fire of charity in the heart.

WASHINGTON IRVING

NOT to understand a treasure's worth,
Till time has stolen away the slightest good,
Is cause of half the poverty we feel,
And makes the world the wilderness it is.

WILLIAM COWPER

IF we love one another, nothing in truth, can harm us, whatever mischances may happen.

HENRY WADSWORTH LONGFELLOW

A MERRY heart doeth good like a medicine.

PROVERBS 17:22

THE wealth of man is the number of things which he loves and blesses, which he is loved and blessed by.

THOMAS CARLYLE

PROSPERITY is the blessing of the Old
    Testament;
Adversity is the blessing of the New.

FRANCIS BACON

THERE is no duty we so much underrate as the duty of being happy.

ROBERT LOUIS STEVENSON

I HEARD the bells on Christmas Day
Their old, familiar carols play,
    And wild and sweet
    The words repeat
Of peace on earth, good-will to men!

HENRY WADSWORTH LONGFELLOW

IT IS in the enjoyment and not in mere possession that makes for happiness.

MICHEL DE MONTAIGNE

BE not forgetful to entertain strangers, for thereby some have entertained angels unawares.

HEBREWS 13:2

COME, bring with a noise,
My merry, merry boys,
The Christmas log to the firing;
While my good dame, she
Bids ye all be free;
And drink to your hearts' desiring.

ROBERT HERRICK

HEAP on more wood! — the wind is chill;
But let it whistle as it will,
We'll keep our Christmas merry still.

SIR WALTER SCOTT

MAY joy come from God above
To all those who Christmas love.

13TH CENTURY CAROL

THE world is so full of a number of things,
I'm sure we should all be as happy as kings.

ROBERT LOUIS STEVENSON

GIVE US, oh, give us, the man who sings at his work! He will do more in the same time, — he will do it better, — he will persevere longer. One is scarcely sensible of fatigue whilst he marches to music. The very stars are said to make harmony as they revolve in their spheres. Wondrous is the strength of cheerfulness, altogether past calculation in its powers of endurance. Efforts, to be permanently useful, must be uniformly joyous, a spirit all sunshine, graceful from very gladness, beautiful because bright. . . . Blessed is he who has found his work; let him ask no other blessedness.

THOMAS CARLYLE

WRITE me as one who loves his fellow men.

LEIGH HUNT

THE blessings of fortune are the lowest; the next are the bodily advantages of strength and health; but the superlative blessings, in fine, are those of the mind.

SIR ROGER L'ESTRANGE

WHOEVER gives a small coin to a poor man has six blessings bestowed upon him, but he who speaks a kind word to him obtains eleven blessings.

TALMUD

I SOMETIMES think we expect too much of Christmas Day. We try to crowd into it the long arrears of kindliness and humanity of the whole year. As for me, I like to take my Christmas a little at a time, all through the year. And thus I drift along into the holidays — let them overtake me unexpectedly — waking up some fine morning and suddenly saying to myself: "Why, this is Christmas Day!"

DAVID GRAYSON

THE art of pleasing requires only the desire.

LORD CHESTERFIELD

FOR he who gives joy to the world is raised higher among men than he who conquers the world.

RICHARD WAGNER

NEVER deny the babies their Christmas! It is the shining seal set upon a year of happiness. Let them believe in Santa Claus, or St. Nicholas, or Kris Kringle, or whatever name the jolly Dutch saint bears in your religion.

MARION HARLAND

To heal divisions, to relieve the oppress'd,
In virtue rich; in blessing others, bless'd.

HOMER

AH, but a man's reach should exceed his grasp,
or what's a heaven for?

ROBERT BROWNING

So now is come our joyfulst feast;
Let every man be jolly.
Each room with ivy leaves is dressed
And every post with holly.

GEORGE WITHER

A LAUGH is worth a hundred groans in any market.

CHARLES LAMB

A FELLOW-FEELING makes one wondrous kind.

DAVID GARRICK

EVERYWHERE, everywhere, Christmas
   tonight!
Christmas in lands of the fir-tree and pine,
Christmas in lands of the palm-tree and vine,
Christmas where snow peaks stand solemn
   and white,
Christmas where cornfields stand sunny and
   bright.
Christmas where children are hopeful and
   gay,
Christmas where old men are patient and
   gray,
Christmas where peace, like a dove in his
   flight,
Broods o'er brave men in the thick of the
   fight;
Everywhere, everywhere, Christmas
   tonight!

PHILLIPS BROOKS

I HAVE always thought of Christmas time, when it has come round, apart from the veneration due to its sacred name and origin, if anything belonging to it can be apart from that — as a good time; a kind, forgiving, charitable, pleasant time.

CHARLES DICKENS

A MAN's best things are nearest him, lie close about his feet.

RICHARD MONCKTON MILNES

'TIS expectation makes a blessing dear, Heaven were not heaven, if we knew what
   it were.

JOHN MILTON

RING out the old, ring in the new . . . Ring out the false, ring in the true.

ALFRED, LORD TENNYSON

THE blessing of the Lord, it maketh rich, and He addeth no sorrow with it.

PROVERBS 10:22

AND numerous indeed are the hearts to which Christmas brings a brief season of happiness and enjoyment. How many families whose members have been dispersed and scattered far and wide, in the restless struggle of life, are then reunited, and meet once again in that happy state of companionship and mutual good-will, which is a source of such pure and unalloyed delight, and one so incompatible with the cares and sorrows of the world that the religious belief of the most civilized nations, and the rude traditions of the roughest savages, alike number it among the first days of a future state of existence, provided for the blest and happy! How many old recollections, and how many, dormant sympathies, Christmas-time awakens!

We write these words now, many miles distant from the spot at which, year after year, we met in that day, a merry and joyous circle. Many of the hearts that throbbed so gaily then, have ceased to beat; . . . and yet the old house, the room, the merry voices and smiling faces, the jest, the laugh, the most minute and trivial circumstance connected with those happy meetings, crowd upon our mind at each recurrence of the season, as if the last assemblage had been but yesterday. Happy, happy Christmas, that can win us back to the delusions of our childish days, recall to the old man the pleasures of his youth, and transport the traveler back to his own fireside and quiet home!

CHARLES DICKENS

For the few hours of life allotted me,
Give me (Great God) but bread and liberty,
I'll beg no more; if more thou'rt pleased to
    give,
I'll thankfully that overplus receive;
If beyond this no more be freely sent,
I'll thank for this, and go away content.

ABRAHAM COWLEY

MEMORY is the power to gather roses in winter.

ANONYMOUS

BLESSED be mirthfulness; it is God's medicine – one of the renovators of the world. – Everybody ought to bathe in it. Grim care, moroseness, anxiety, – all this rust of life, ought to be scoured off by the oil of mirth. It is better than emery. Every man ought to rub himself with it. A man without mirth is like a wagon without springs, in which one is caused disagreeably to jolt by every pebble over which it runs.

HENRY WARD BEECHER

AND more than wisdom, more than wealth, – A merry heart that laughs at care.

HENRY HART MILMAN

LET us therefore follow after the things which make for peace.

ROMANS 14:19

THE feeling of friendship is like that of being comfortably filled with roast beef; love, like being enlivened with champagne.

SAMUEL JOHNSON

27

MIRTHFULNESS is in the mind, and you cannot get it out. It is the blessed spirit that God has set in the mind to dust it, to enliven its dark places, and to drive asceticism, like a foul fiend, out of the back-door. It is just as good, in its place, as conscience or veneration. Praying can no more be made a substitute for smiling than smiling can for praying.

HENRY WARD BEECHER

O LITTLE town of Bethlehem!
　　How still we see thee lie;
Above thy deep and dreamless sleep
　　The silent stars go by;
Yet in thy dark streets shineth
　　The everlasting Light;
The hopes and fears of all the years
　　Are met in thee to-night.

PHILLIPS BROOKS

THE essence of humor is sensibility; warm tender fellow-feeling with all forms of existence.

THOMAS CARLYLE

NOTHING raises the price of a blessing like its removal; whereas it was its continuance which should have taught us its value. There are three requisites to the proper enjoyment of earthly blessings, — a thankful reflection on the goodness of the Giver, a deep sense of our unworthiness, a recollection of the uncertainty of long possessing them. The first would make us grateful; the second, humble; and the third, moderate.

HANNAH MORE

SEEK love in the pity of others' woe,
In the gentle relief of another's care,
In the darkness of night and the winter's
   snow;
In the naked and outcast — seek love there.

WILLIAM BLAKE

THE good things of life are not to be had singly, but come to us with a mixture; like a school-boy's holiday, with a task affixed to the tails of it.

CHARLES LAMB

CHEERFUL looks make every dish a feast; and it is that which crowns a welcome.

PHILIP MASSINGER

CHRISTMAS is coming, the geese are getting
  fat,
Please to put a penny in the old man's hat;
If you haven't got a penny, a ha' penny will
  do,
If you haven't got a ha' penny, God bless you!
Beggar's Rhyme—ANONYMOUS

BLESSED is not the reward of virtue but virtue itself.

BENEDICT SPINOZA

IT IS not doing the thing we like to do, but liking the thing we have to do, that makes life blessed.

JOHANN WOLFGANG VON GOETHE

GIVE what you have. To someone, it may be better than you dare to think.

HENRY WADSWORTH LONGFELLOW

CHARITIES that soothe and heal and bless lie
scattered at the feet of men like flowers.

WILLIAM WORDSWORTH

ANNOUNCED by all the trumpets of the sky,
Arrives the snow, and, driving o'er the fields,
Seems nowhere to alight; the whited air
Hides hills and woods, the river, and the
    heaven,
And veils the farmhouse at the garden's end.
The sled and traveler stopped, the courier's
    feet
Delayed, all friends shut out, the housemates
    sit
Around the radiant fireplace, enclosed
In a tumultuous privacy of storm.

RALPH WALDO EMERSON

WHENEVER evil befalls us, we ought to ask
ourselves, after the first suffering, how we
can turn it into good. So shall we take occa-
sion, from one bitter root, to raise perhaps
many flowers.

LEIGH HUNT

THERE never was any heart truly great and generous, that was not also tender and compassionate.

ROBERT SOUTH

GOD taught mankind on that first Christmas
  day
What 'twas to be a man; to give, not take;
To serve, not rule; to nourish, not devour;
To help, not crush; if need, to die, not live.

CHARLES KINGSLEY

FOR somehow, not only at Christmas, but all
  the long year through,
The joy that you give to others is the joy that
  comes back to you.

JOHN GREENLEAF WHITTIER

THE comforter's head never aches.

GEORGE HERBERT

To the man who himself strives earnestly,
God also lends a helping hand.

AESCHYLUS

33

God made both tears and laughter, and both for kind purposes; for as laughter enables mirth and surprise to breathe freely, so tears enable sorrow to vent itself patiently.

Leigh Hunt

It came upon the midnight clear,
That glorious song of old,
From Angels bending near the earth
To touch their harps of gold;
"Peace on the earth, good will to men
From Heaven's all gracious King."
The world in solemn stillness lay
To hear the angels sing.

Edmund Hamilton Sears

Words are the voice of the heart.

Confucius

He who helps a child helps humanity with an immediateness which no other help given to human creature in any other stage of human life can possibly give again.

Phillips Brooks

How often it is difficult to be wisely charitable — to do good without multiplying the sources of evil. To give alms is nothing unless you give thought also. It is written, not "blessed is he that feedeth the poor," but "blessed is he that considereth the poor." A little thought and a little kindness are often worth more than a great deal of money.

JOHN RUSKIN

THE first Noël the angels did say
Was to certain poor shepherds
In fields as they lay;
In fields where they lay
Keeping their sheep,
In a cold winter's night
That was so deep.
Noël, Noël, Noël, Noël.
Born is the King of Israel.

TRADITIONAL

As you receive the stranger, so you receive your God.

JOHANN KASPAR LAVATER

LAUGHTER, while it lasts, slackens and unbraces the mind, weakens the faculties, and causes a kind of remissness and dissolution in all the powers of the soul; and thus far it may be looked upon as a weakness in the composition of human nature. But if we consider the frequent reliefs we receive from it, and how often it breaks the gloom which is apt to depress the mind and damp our spirits, with transient, unexpected gleams of joy, one would take care not to grow too wise for so great a pleasure of life.

JOSEPH ADDISON

MUSIC is well said to be the speech of angels.

THOMAS CARLYLE

SPEND your brief moment according to nature's law, and serenely greet the journey's end as an olive falls when it is ripe, blessing the branch that bore it, and giving thanks to the tree that gave it life.

MARCUS AURELIUS

WHEN the day returns, call us up with morning faces and with morning hearts, eager to labor, happy if happiness be our portion, and if the day be marked for sorrow, strong to endure.

ROBERT LOUIS STEVENSON

HE who blesses most is blest:
  And God and man shall own his worth
Who toils to leave as his bequest
  An added beauty to the earth.

JOHN GREENLEAF WHITTIER

JOY to the world! the Lord is come:
Let earth receive her King;
Let ev'ry heart prepare Him room;
And heav'n and nature sing, . . .

ISAAC WATTS

FRIENDSHIP is the nearest thing we know to what religion is. God is love, and, to make religion akin to friendship is simply to give it the highest expression conceivable to man.

JOHN RUSKIN

NEVER lose an opportunity of seeing anything that is beautiful; for beauty is God's handwriting — a wayside sacrament. Welcome it in every fair face, in every fair sky, in every fair flower, and thank God for it as a cup of blessing.

RALPH WALDO EMERSON

I'D LOAD a wagon with caramels
And a candy of every kind,
And buy all the almond and pecan nuts
And taffy that I could find;
And barrels and barrels of oranges
I'd scatter right in the way,
So the children would find them the very
    first thing
When they wake on Christmas Day.

EUGENE FIELD

NOT what we give, but what we share,
For the gift without the giver is bare;
Who gives himself with his alms feeds three,
Himself, his hungering neighbor and Me.

JAMES RUSSELL LOWELL

OH, my friend, is it the settled rule of life that we are to accept nothing not expensive? It is not so settled for me. That which is freest, cheapest, seems somehow more valuable than anything I pay for; that which is given, better than that which is bought; that which passes between you and me in the glance of an eye, a touch of the hand, is better than minted money!

DAVID GRAYSON

THE earth has grown old with its burdens of
        care,
    But at Christmas it always is young;
The heart of the jewel burns lustrous and fair,
And its soul, full of music, breaks forth on
        the air
    When the song of the angels is sung.

PHILLIPS BROOKS

ONE has only to grow older to become more tolerant. I see no wrong that I might not have committed myself.

JOHANN WOLFGANG VON GOETHE

PEACE was the first thing the angels sang. Peace is the mark of the sons of God. Peace is the nurse of love. Peace is the mother of unity. Peace is the rest of blessed souls. Peace is the dwelling place of eternity.

LEO THE GREAT

I ASK and wish not to appear
    More beauteous, rich or gay:
Lord make me wiser every year,
    And better every day.

CHARLES LAMB

A HEART that can feel for another's woe,
And share his joys with a genial glow;
With sympathies large enough to enfold
All men as brothers, is better than gold.

ABRAM JOSEPH RYAN

WE love music for the buried hopes, the garnered memories, the tender feelings it can summon at a touch.

LETITIA ELIZABETH LANDON

You were made for enjoyment, and the world was filled with things which you will enjoy, unless you are too proud to be pleased with them, or too grasping to care for what you can not turn to other account than mere delight.

JOHN RUSKIN

HE IS the happiest, be he king or peasant, who finds peace in his home.

JOHANN WOLFGANG VON GOETHE

WHAT can I give Him,
Poor as I am?
If I were a shepherd
I would bring Him a lamb —
If I were a Wise Man
I would do my part —
Yet what I can, I give Him,
Give my heart.

CHRISTINA ROSSETTI

SWEET is the smile of home; the mutual look,
When hearts are of each other sure.

JOHN KEBLE

MAKE yourselves nests of pleasant thoughts. None of us yet know, for none of us have been taught in early youth, what fairy palaces we may build of beautiful thought — proof against all adversity. Bright fancies, satisfied memories, noble histories, faithful sayings, treasure-houses of precious and restful thoughts, which care cannot disturb, nor pain make gloomy, nor poverty take away from us — houses built without hands, for our souls to live in.

JOHN RUSKIN

BACK of the loaf is the snowy flour,
    And back of the flour the mill,
And back of the mill is the wheat and the
        shower,
    And the sun and the Father's will.

MALTBIE DAVENPORT BABCOCK

To receive a present handsomely and in a right spirit, even when you have none to give in return, is to give one in return.

LEIGH HUNT

WHEN there is room in the heart, there is room in the house.

DANISH PROVERB

'Twas the night before Christmas, when all
    through the house
Not a creature was stirring, not even a mouse;
The stockings were hung by the chimney
    with care,
In hopes that St. Nicholas soon would be
    there;

.   .   .   .   .

When out on the lawn there arose such a
    clatter,
I sprang from my bed to see what was the
    matter.
As I drew in my head, and was turning
    around,
Down the chimney St. Nicholas came with a
    bound.

.   .   .   .   .

He spoke not a word, but went straight to
    his work,

And filled all the stockings; then turned with
    a jerk,

          .   .   .   .   .

But I heard him exclaim, ere he drove out of
    sight,
"Happy Christmas to all, and to all a good-
    night!"

CLEMENT CLARKE MOORE

THE only gift is a portion of thyself.

RALPH WALDO EMERSON

IT's merry when friends meet.

JOHN CLARKE

A GOOD laugh is sunshine in a house.

WILLIAM MAKEPEACE THACKERAY

ABOVE all, let us never forget that an act of
goodness is in itself an act of happiness. It is
the flower of a long inner life of joy and con-
tentment; it tells of peaceful hours and days
on the sunniest heights of our soul.

MAURICE MAETERLINCK

THE joyfulness of a man prolongeth his days.

ECCLESIASTICUS 30:22

So all night long the storm roared on:
The morning broke without a sun;
In tiny spherule traced with lines
Of Nature's geometric signs,
In starry flake and pellicle,
All day the hoary meteor fell;
And, when the second morning shone,
We looked upon a world unknown,
On nothing we could call our own.
Around the glistening wonder bent
The blue walls of the firmament,
No cloud above, no earth below, —
A universe of sky and snow!

. . . . .

Shut in from all the world without,
We sat the clean-winged hearth about,
Content to let the north-wind roar
In baffled rage at pane and door,
While the red logs before us beat
The frost-line back with tropic heat; . . .

JOHN GREENLEAF WHITTIER

CHRISTMAS TIME! That man must be a misanthrope indeed, in whose breast something like a jovial feeling is not roused — in whose mind some pleasant associations are not awakened — by the recurrence of Christmas. There are people who will tell you that Christmas is not to them what it used to be. . . . Never heed such dismal reminiscences. There are few men who have lived long enough in the world, who cannot call up such thoughts any day in the year. Then do not select the merriest of the three hundred and sixty-five, for your doleful recollections, but draw your chair nearer the blazing fire — fill the glass and send round the song . . . and thank God it's no worse. . . . Reflect upon your present blessings — of which every man has many — not on your past misfortunes, of which all men have some. Fill your glass again, with a merry face and contented heart. Our life on it, but your Christmas shall be merry, and your new year a happy one!

CHARLES DICKENS

WHO rises from Prayer a better man, his prayer is answered.

GEORGE MEREDITH

MORE things are wrought by prayer
Than this world dreams of. Wherefore, let
   thy voice
Rise like a fountain for me night and day.
For what are men better than sheep and goats
That nourish a blind life within the brain,
If, knowing God, they lift not hands of
   prayer
Both for themselves and those who call them
   friend?
For so the whole round earth is every way
Bound by gold chains about the feet of God.

ALFRED, LORD TENNYSON

BLESSED are they who have the gift of making friends, for it is one of God's best gifts. It involves many things, but above all, the power of going out of one's self, and appreciating whatever is noble and loving in another.

THOMAS HUGHES

LET everyone be himself, and not try to be someone else. God, who looked on the world He had made and said it was all good, made each of us to be just what our own gifts and faculties fit us to be. Be that and do that and so be contented. Reverence, also, each other's gifts; do not quarrel with me because I am not you, and I will do the same. God made your brother as well as yourself. He made you, perhaps, to be bright; he made him slow; he made you practical; he made him speculative; he made one strong and another weak, one tough and another tender; but the same God made us all. Let us not torment each other because we are not all alike, but believe that God knew best what he was doing in making us so different. So will the best harmony come out of seeming discords, the best affection out of differences, the best life out of struggle, and the best work will be done when each does his own work, and lets everyone else do and be what God made him for.

JAMES FREEMAN CLARKE

ALL I have seen teaches me to trust the Creator for all I have not seen.

RALPH WALDO EMERSON

GIVE us men. A time like this demands
Strong minds, great hearts, true faith, and
 ready hands;
Men whom the lust of office does not kill;
Men whom the spoils of office cannot buy;
Men who possess opinions and a will;
Men who have honor; men who will not lie;
Men who can stand before a demagogue
And damn his treacherous flatterings without
 winking;
Tall men, sun-crowned, who live above the
 fog
In public duty and in private thinking.

JOSIAH GILBERT HOLLAND

SUCH a winter eve. Now for a mellow fire, some old poet's page, or else serene philosophy.

HENRY DAVID THOREAU

It is good to be children sometimes, and never better than at Christmas, when its mighty Founder was a child Himself.

CHARLES DICKENS

On the twelfth day of Christmas
My true love sent to me
Twelve drummers drumming,
Eleven pipers piping,
Ten lords a-leaping,
Nine ladies dancing,
Eight maids a-milking,
Seven swans a-swimming,
Six geese a-laying,
Five golden rings...
Four calling birds,
Three French hens,
Two turtledoves
And a partridge in a pear tree.

OLD ENGLISH CAROL *for the Twelve Days*
between Christmas and Epiphany

MUSIC is the universal language of mankind.

HENRY WADSWORTH LONGFELLOW

MAY I be no man's enemy, and may I be the friend of that which is eternal and abides. May I never quarrel with those nearest me; and if I do, may I be reconciled quickly. May I never devise evil against any man; if any devise evil against me, may I escape un-injured and without the need of hurting him. May I love, seek, and attain only that which is good. May I wish for all men's happiness and envy none.

EUSEBIUS

IF ever household affections and love are graceful things, they are graceful in the poor. The ties that bind the wealthy and the proud to home may be forged on earth, but those which link the poor man to his humble hearth are of the truer metal and bear the stamp of Heaven. . . . His household gods are of flesh and blood, with no alloy of silver, gold, or precious stone; he has no property but in the affections of his own heart.

CHARLES DICKENS

54

HE is a wise man who does not grieve for the things which he has not, but rejoices for those which he has.

EPICTETUS

CHRISTMAS hath a darkness
Brighter than the blazing noon;
Christmas hath a chilliness
Warmer than the heart of June;
Christmas hath a beauty
Lovelier than the world can show.

CHRISTINA ROSSETTI

FOR blessings ever wait on virtuous deeds,
And though a late, a sure reward succeeds.

WILLIAM CONGREVE

BLESSED are the joymakers.

NATHANIEL PARKER WILLIS

SURELY it is not true blessedness to be free from sorrow while there is sorrow and sin in the world; sorrow is then a part of love, and love does not seek to throw it off.

GEORGE ELIOT

CHRISTMAS is the most human and kindly of seasons, as fully penetrated and irradiated with the feeling of human brotherhood, which is the essential spirit of Christianity, as the month of June with sunshine and the balmy breath of roses.

GEORGE WILLIAM CURTIS

THE greatest blessing is created and enjoyed at the same moment.

EPICURUS

HE who receives a benefit with gratitude, repays the first installment on his debt.

SENECA

THE wise man will make more opportunities than he finds.

FRANCIS BACON

IT IS one of the most beautiful compensations of this life that no man can sincerely try to help another without helping himself.

RALPH WALDO EMERSON

I DIMLY guess, from blessings known, of greater out of sight.

JOHN GREENLEAF WHITTIER

LAUGHTER is the joyous universal evergreen of life.

ABRAHAM LINCOLN

AH, how good it feels! The hand of an old friend.

HENRY WADSWORTH LONGFELLOW

AT Christmas play, and make good cheer,
For Christmas comes but once a year.

THOMAS TUSSER

To a young heart everything is fun.

CHARLES DICKENS

THE very society of joy redoubles it; so that, while it lights upon my friend it rebounds upon myself, and the brighter his candle burns the more easily will it light mine.

ROBERT SOUTH

GOD, who hast given us the love of women and the friendship of men, keep alive in our hearts the sense of old fellowship and tenderness; make offences to be forgotten and services remembered; protect those whom we love in all things and follow them with kindnesses, so that they may lead simple and unsuffering lives, and in the end die easily with quiet minds.

ROBERT LOUIS STEVENSON

THERE is something in the very season of the year that gives a charm to the festivity of Christmas. At other times we derive a great portion of our pleasures from the mere beauties of nature. Our feelings sally forth and dissipate themselves over the sunny landscape, and we "live abroad and everywhere." The song of the bird, the murmur of the stream, the breathing fragrance of spring, the soft voluptuousness of summer, the golden pomp of autumn, earth with its mantle of refreshing green, and heaven with its deep delicious blue and its cloudy magnificence — all fill us with mute but exquisite delight, and we revel in the luxury of mere sensation. But in the depth of winter, when nature lies despoiled of every charm and wrapped in her shroud of sheeted snow, we turn for gratifications to moral sources.

The dreariness and desolation of the landscape, the short and gloomy days and darksome nights, while they circumscribe our wanderings, shut in our feelings also from rambling abroad, and make us more kindly disposed for the pleasure of the social circle. Our thoughts are more concentrated; our friendly sympathies more aroused. We feel more sensibly the charm of each other's society, and are brought more closely together by dependence on each other for enjoyment. Heart calls unto heart; and we draw our pleasures from the deep wells of loving kindness which lie in the quiet recesses of our bosoms, and which, when resorted to, furnish forth the pure element of domestic felicity.

Washington Irving

LOVE and friendship are the discoveries of ourselves in others, and our delight in the recognition; and in men as in books, we only know that, the parallel of which we have in ourselves.   ALEXANDER SMITH

BLESSED are the poor in spirit: for theirs is the kingdom of heaven.

Blessed are they that mourn: for they shall be comforted.

Blessed are the meek: for they shall inherit the earth.

Blessed are they which do hunger and thirst after righteousness: for they shall be filled.

Blessed are the merciful: for they shall obtain mercy.

Blessed are the pure in heart: for they shall see God.

Blessed are the peacemakers: for they shall be called the children of God.

Blessed are they which are persecuted for righteousness' sake: for theirs is the king-dom of Heaven.

60

Blessed are ye, when men shall revile you,
and persecute you, and shall say all man-
ner of evil against you falsely, for my sake.
Rejoice, and be exceeding glad: for great is
your reward in heaven: for so persecuted
they the prophets which were before you.

St. Matthew 5:3-12

'Mid pleasures and palaces though we may
    roam,
Be it ever so humble, there's no place like
    home;
A charm from the sky seems to hallow us
    there,
Which, seek through the world, is ne'er met
    with elsewhere.
  Home, home, sweet, sweet home!

John Howard Payne

Over the winter glaciers I see the summer
glow, and through the wide-piled snowdrift
the warm rosebuds below.

Ralph Waldo Emerson

To make some nook of God's Creation a little fruitfuller, better, more worthy of God; to make some human hearts a little wiser, man-fuller, happier, — more blessed, less accursed! It is work for a God.

THOMAS CARLYLE

"WHAT means this glory round our feet,"
    The Magi mused, "more bright than
        morn?"
And voices chanted clear and sweet,
    "Today the Prince of Peace is born!"

"What means that star," the Shepherds said,
    "That brightens through the rocky glen?"
And angels, answering overhead,
    Sang, "Peace on earth, good-will to men!"

JAMES RUSSELL LOWELL

IT IS more blessed to give than to receive.

ACTS 20:35

IT IS a fine seasoning for joy to think of those we love.

JEAN BAPTISTE MOLIÈRE

THERE never was such a goose. Bob said he didn't believe there ever was such a goose cooked. Its tenderness and flavor, size and cheapness, were the themes of universal admiration . . . Then the pudding was out of the copper . . . Oh, a wonderful pudding! Bob Cratchit said, and calmly too, that he regarded it as the greatest success achieved by Mrs. Cratchit since their marriage . . . Then all the Cratchit family drew round the hearth, in what Bob Cratchit called a circle . . . ; and at Bob Cratchit's elbow stood the family display of glass. Two tumblers, and a custard-cup without a handle.

These held the hot stuff from the jug, however, as well as golden goblets would have done; and Bob served it with beaming looks, while the chestnuts on the fire sputtered and cracked noisily. Then Bob proposed:

"A Merry Christmas to us all my dears. God bless us!"

"God bless us every one!" said Tiny Tim, the last of all.

CHARLES DICKENS